TOOS! GOES UPTOWN!

KAREN L. BELCIGLIO   TRACEY TOLBERT   KYLE F. ANDERSON

ISBN: 1479120375
ISBN 13: 9781479120376
Library of Congress Control Number: 2012914985
CreateSpace Independent Publishing Platform North Charleston, South Carolina

Every adventure begins with your imagination

6/18/14

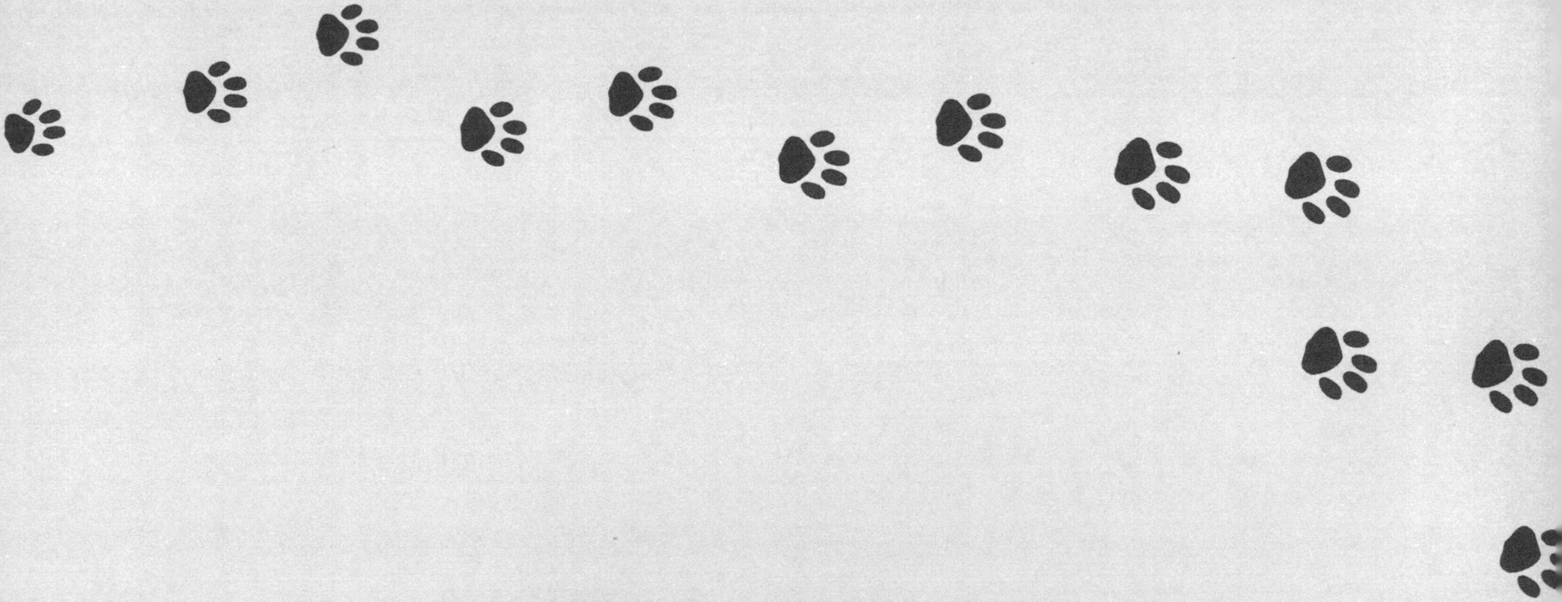

This Book Belongs to:

Hey! I'm Toos. You say it like *moose* with a T.

No, I'm not the human—that's John.
(Goofy-looking hat, I know.)

I'm the cat. I'm a guy calico cat, which is really rare.
Cats like me are lucky: whenever I've done something
bad, something good comes out of it.

We live in Charlotte; John says it's a town for cats.

So, this is my life.

I sleep, eat, play with catnip toys, and glare at the birds outside the window. Glaring at the birds is my favorite part.

Yep, it's hard work. And even lucky cats like me get bored with working so hard at the same jobs all the time.

So I tore up some of John's papers. I figured he was going to put them in the noisy shredder anyway. I was helping - saving him the trouble, you know?

When John found my mess, he yelled, "You furry fuzzball! That was important! ARRRRRGH!"
He threw his goofy hat on the floor. At least that was an improvement.

4

One day when John went to get the paper, he left the door open.

I thought: Let me check out all these other Charlotte cats. After all, John didn't seem to appreciate my help. And if this is a town for cats surely I'd find one to be friends and hang with.

So I bolted out the door.

John went nuts! He called my name and tried to catch me.

Poor guy. Slow as molasses. He's no cat, that's for sure.

I ran around the corner and there was a bus waiting.

John was right. Charlotte is a town for cats.

The bus said so. "CATS." Right on the side. Awesome.

When I got on, the lady driver asked me for money.

Huh?

I gave her my best bird glare and thought, "Look, lady, I'm a cat on a CATS bus. I ride free." She got the message, because she left me alone after that.

I climbed a seat and looked around, searching for my new feline friend. But there were no other cats on the bus. Hmmm. Where could they be?

The bus rumbled along, and my ears twitched at the sound of a familiar word. "Yeah, Bobcats!" said a guy.

"Dude, this ball game will be awesome!" his friend responded. They were headed uptown to see them play.

Bobcats? I wondered. Bobcats were supposed to be wild and fierce. I didn't know they played with balls.

Maybe that's where all the other cats were. Not on the bus; at the Bobcats game! I was going uptown.

I followed the dudes off the bus and into a huge arena.

But there were no bobcats.

None.

And no cats either. Just a bunch of crazy people jumping and shouting and not watching where they were stepping.

Ouch! I was outta there.

I scooted out of that stadium, stuck my tail up in the air, and walked on down the block.

Before long, I approached a corner where humans kept pointing up at something.

"Look! It's the Firebird! How fantastic!" they said.

It seemed like a good place to get a look around and maybe give me a chance to spot those other cats. So I climbed on top. But there was no fire. And no bird. Strange.

And even stranger? Still no cats!

Disappointed, I climbed off and continued down the street.

Hey. *Hey!* Now *there* was a *cat!* A *huge* cat!

It had glittering green eyes, strong rippling muscles, big wicked claws, and long pointy teeth. A panther! He was as cool as me.

"Hey, how's it going?" I asked him, all casual like. His expression didn't change.

"I like your claws. I've got sharp claws too!" I jumped up high until I reached him. "See?" I showed him my claws. I gave his leg a soft scratch. *Eek!*

I leaped back to the ground. Cold metal! This was no panther. He was just a statue!

A really awesome statue, but statues aren't cats. I mean, they can look like cats, but they're not cats.

And statues aren't human either.

Great. What was I supposed to do now?

I was a cat in a cat-less town. I missed my human, John. Plus I was hungry and ready for a nap.

And just in time, there came the wacky CATS bus with no cats in it. Now if that lady bus driver would just stop asking me for money.

Seriously?

At least I was on my way home.

When I got there, John was really, really happy to see me. I let him pick me up. "Yeah, purr it up, fuzzball," he said.

John told me that I was a lucky cat after all, since I had gone out exploring and searching for some friends on my own and had come back safe. And I had made something good happen out of something bad. When he had been out looking for me, he met a cool new friend—Kyle.

That's Kyle in the blue shirt. Kyle's an artist, and he likes cats too. At least one of us found a new friend today.

I'm not sure when I'll go back out. There may have been only one great cat uptown—me—but for now I think I'll stick with John. Even if he does wear goofy hats.

After all, someone's gotta glare at those birds.

Made in the USA
San Bernardino, CA
10 June 2014